GW00863696

I am in park

written by Jay Dale

illustrated by Michelle Dybing

I am in the park.

Here is a dog.

I am in the garden.

Here is a butterfly.

I am in the bath.

Here is a duck.

I am in the sandpit.

Here is a truck.

I am in the pool.

Here is a ball.

I am in the playhouse.

Here is a dinosaur.

I am in the shop.

Here is a cake.

I am in the boat.
Here is a fish.